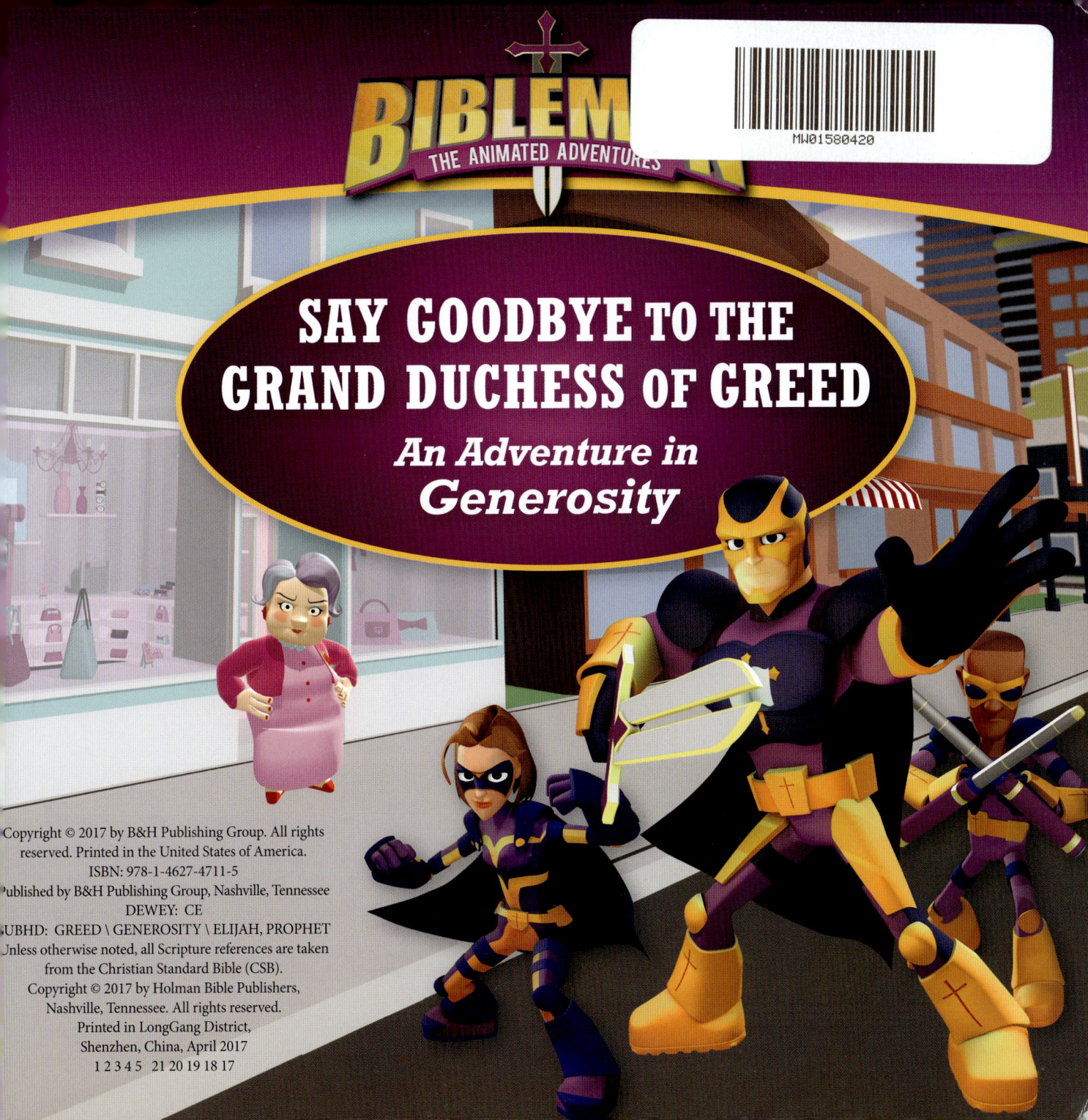

BIBLEMAN
THE ANIMATED ADVENTURES

SAY GOODBYE TO THE GRAND DUCHESS OF GREED
An Adventure in Generosity

Copyright © 2017 by B&H Publishing Group. All rights reserved. Printed in the United States of America.
ISBN: 978-1-4627-4711-5
Published by B&H Publishing Group, Nashville, Tennessee
DEWEY: CE
SUBHD: GREED \ GENEROSITY \ ELIJAH, PROPHET
Unless otherwise noted, all Scripture references are taken from the Christian Standard Bible (CSB).
Copyright © 2017 by Holman Bible Publishers, Nashville, Tennessee. All rights reserved.
Printed in LongGang District, Shenzhen, China, April 2017
1 2 3 4 5   21 20 19 18 17

One day, two sisters were asking for donations for the church fund-raiser, but one shop owner wanted to *take* money instead. She saw the girls coming and came up with a plan to get them to buy something.

She placed a shiny phone case on the counter and blew some sparkling greed-dust onto it.

The sisters entered the shop with high hopes.

"Welcome to Designer Delights," said the shop owner. "My name is Gweneth Reed. How can I help you girls?"

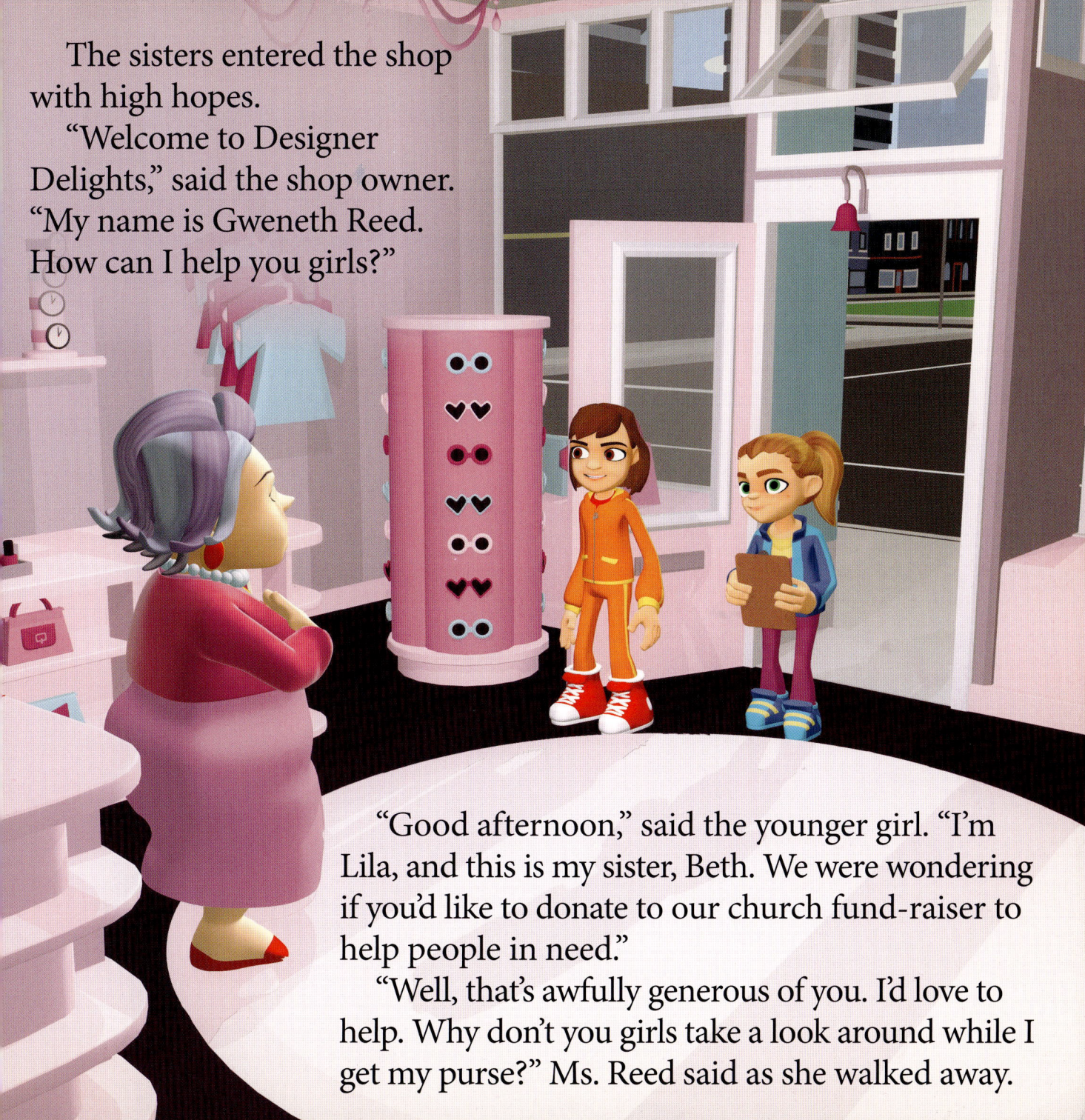

"Good afternoon," said the younger girl. "I'm Lila, and this is my sister, Beth. We were wondering if you'd like to donate to our church fund-raiser to help people in need."

"Well, that's awfully generous of you. I'd love to help. Why don't you girls take a look around while I get my purse?" Ms. Reed said as she walked away.

Lila saw the phone case on the counter. "Wow! Look how pretty this case is. I saw one like it in a magazine. I don't just want this case, I need it!" she said with a twinkle in her eyes from the sparkling greed-dust.

Beth cautioned her sister. "I don't know, Lila. It sure is beautiful, but it's thirty dollars!"

Just then, Ms. Reed returned. "I'm sorry, girls. I can't find my checkbook anywhere. But I see someone has found a new phone case," she said with a smile at Lila.

Lila looked sad. "It's really pretty, but Beth's right. It's too expensive."

"Well, my dear, fashion comes with a price," Ms. Reed said. "It takes a special girl to pull off such a special case."

Lila's eyes twinkled again as the greed-dust filled her with greed.

"We should be going now," Beth said when she saw Lila's eyes light up. "Thank you for your time, Ms. Reed. Maybe you can come by the fund-raiser at the church tomorrow to give your donation."

"Oh, I'm afraid I won't be able to make it. Why don't you come back by on your way, Lila, and I can give you the check then? I'll save this phone case for you, just in case," Ms. Reed added in a whisper.

As the girls left the shop, Ms. Reed blew more sparkling greed-dust onto Lila.

"I can't stop thinking about that phone case," Lila said as they walked home.

"Where are you going to get thirty dollars?" Beth asked. "Wait, you're not thinking of using the money you pledged for the fund-raiser, are you?"

Lila looked guilty. "You don't understand. You get new stuff all the time."

"This isn't about wanting something new," Beth reminded her. "It's about generosity and keeping your promises. This money is going toward giving food and clothes to people who can't afford it, not a case for someone else's phone."

Lila yelled at her sister. "It's my money, Beth! Why should I give it all away? I can buy the case and still have some left over to donate. I should be able to spend my money however I want."

Lila stormed off, leaving Beth to follow her home in silence.

That night, Lila couldn't stop thinking about the phone case. She grabbed her money and counted it.

On the way to the fund-raiser the next day, Lila stopped at Designer Delights. "Hello, Ms. Reed. I was wondering if you had that donation," Lila said slowly.

"That's not really why you're here, is it?" Ms. Reed said.

"Well, maybe not the only reason. I want this case," Lila admitted. "But it's too expensive. I was wondering if you could give me a deal."

"Look, hun," Ms. Reed replied. "Designer items tell you what to pay, not the other way around."

Lila pulled her jar out of her backpack. "This is the money I pledged to donate."

"Oh, I almost forgot," Ms. Reed said, pulling out a tube of lipstick. "Here's my little gift to all my customers. A pretty girl like you *needs* pretty things." Lila put on the sparkling, ruby lipstick filled with greed-dust.

"You deserve them too," Ms. Reed continued. "You've donated your time to this fund-raiser; you shouldn't have to donate your money too."

"You're right. I do deserve nice things!" Lila chanted.

"Well, you've got more than enough money here," Ms. Reed said as she opened the jar.

At the Bibleteam HQ, the Bibleteam was having fun with a taste test of Cypher's crazy Slush EZ flavor combinations. Suddenly, they got an alert of enemy activity. The location was Designer Delights.

"That's only a block away from the fund-raiser today," Melody said.
"Who is the shop owner, Cypher?" Biblegirl asked.
"It's listed as unknown," he replied with a frown.

"Looks like we'll have to find out for ourselves," Bibleman said. "To the Biblevan!"

Back at the shop, Lila smiled as Ms. Reed handed her the receipt. Lila picked up her backpack and turned to leave.

"Oh, wait! I almost forgot," Ms. Reed said quickly. "This wallet just arrived today. I'll give you a deal for today only—half price on the wallet so you can have a matching set."

"Thank you for the offer," Lila said as her smile faded, "but that would take the rest of my money."

"Just think about it," Ms. Reed responded. She blew another handful of greed-dust on Lila as she left.

Ms. Reed spoke to herself. "That, my dear Lila, is why they call me the Grand Duchess of Greed!"

She let out an evil laugh . . . until she saw the Biblevan pull up in front of her shop! She pretended to read as the Bibleteam entered the store, ready for action.

The Grand Duchess acted surprised. "Oh! My heavens, you startled me. Hey, aren't you that Bibleman fellow everyone's been talking about?"

"Yes, ma'am," he responded. "Are you the shop owner?"

"Well, yes, I am," she answered.

"Our scanners picked up enemy activity at this location," Bibleman said. "Have you noticed anything out of the ordinary?"

"Enemy activity!?" The Grand Duchess sounded shocked. "I'm not sure what you mean, but no. Just business as usual."

"Do you mind if we have a look around, just to be safe?" Bibleman asked.
"Of course not. Better safe than sorry, I always say," she replied.
The Bibleteam searched for clues but didn't find anything.
"Sorry for the interruption, Ms. Reed," Bibleman said, picking up a business card. The Bibleteam left the shop confused.

"I don't understand," Cypher said. "This is the exact spot the sensors said. They've never been wrong before."

"Why don't you take the Biblevan back to HQ and run a test on the sensors, Cypher?"

"Sure thing, Bibleman. The sensors will be down for at least half an hour while I run the test, though," Cypher reminded him.

"I know, but if they aren't working right we may as well not have them at all," Bibleman replied.

"In the meantime, we can walk down to the church to see if they need help setting up for the fund-raiser," Melody said.

Lila and Beth were at the church when the Bibleteam arrived. Lila was very excited to see Melody.

"Can I get a picture with you?" Lila asked, pulling out her phone with its new ruby case.

"Of course. Wow, what a pretty case you have. It looks expensive," Melody said.

"Why don't you tell them where you got the money to pay for it?" Beth said with a frown.

"It's my money, and I'll do what I want with it!" Lila snapped, and she stormed out of the room. *I'll show Beth,* she thought.

"Welcome back, Lila," the Grand Duchess said when Lila returned. "I've been expecting you."

Biblegirl and Melody turned to Beth after Lila left the room. "Can you tell us what's going on?" Biblegirl asked.

Beth explained to the Bibleteam what happened at the shop the day before. "I've never seen her like this. Maybe you can get through to her, Biblegirl," Beth pleaded.

"It seems there's more to this shop than meets the eye," Bibleman said.

"But what? There was nothing there except that sweet, old lady," Melody said.

Just then Bibleman noticed pink glitter on Melody's gloves.

"It must have come from Lila's phone case when I touched it a minute ago," Melody said.

"The phone case? I saw the same pink glitter on the counter at the shop," Bibleman mentioned.

"I'll go find Lila," Melody said as she hurried from the room.

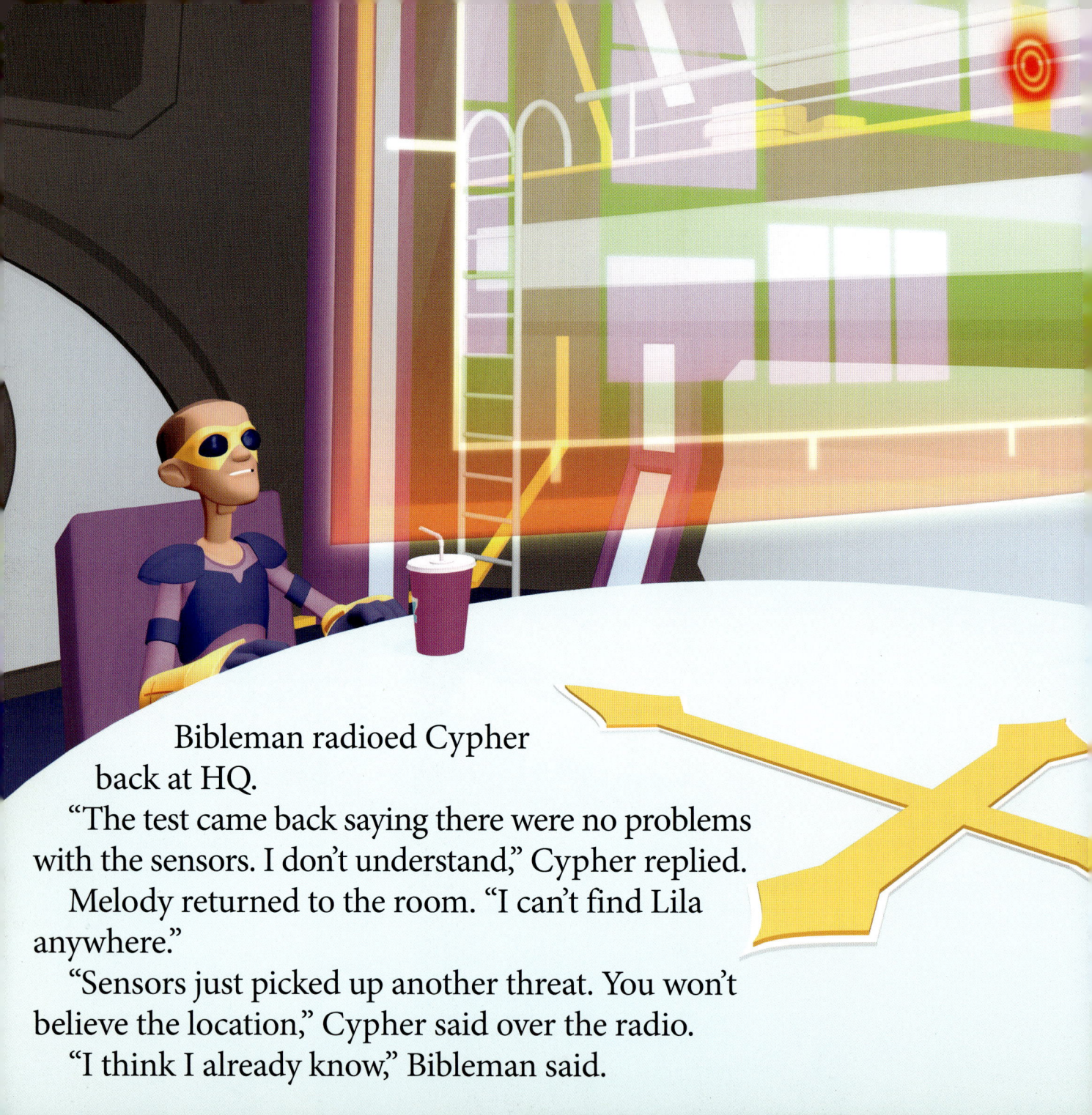

Bibleman radioed Cypher back at HQ.

"The test came back saying there were no problems with the sensors. I don't understand," Cypher replied.

Melody returned to the room. "I can't find Lila anywhere."

"Sensors just picked up another threat. You won't believe the location," Cypher said over the radio.

"I think I already know," Bibleman said.

Lila had just finished buying the ruby wallet when the Bibleteam arrived.

"Bibleman," the Grand Duchess choked. "You're back so soon."

"I see you know our friend Lila," he responded.

"Yes, she's a loyal customer," the Grand Duchess said.

Bibleman turned to Lila. "Beth told us about the money you pledged to the fund-raiser, Lila. You know in Luke 6, Jesus said, 'Give, and it will be given to you. . . . For with the measure you use, it will be measured back to you.'"

Melody shared the story of Elijah and the widow. "God told Elijah to ask a widow for water and bread, but the widow was very poor and said she only had enough for her and her son. Elijah told her to give him bread first and then God would bless her."

"The widow was discouraged, but she followed Elijah's instructions. She gave Elijah bread first. Then she found that God had indeed blessed her. She had plenty of ingredients to make bread for many more days. The widow's faith and trust teach us to be generous and put others before ourselves."

"I was so selfish," Lila said. "Other people need this money more than I do. I'd like to return these for a refund, Ms. Reed."

The Grand Duchess couldn't believe it. Lila's desire to be generous made the greed-dust stop working. The Grand Duchess knew she had been defeated. "This won't be the last you'll see of me, Bibleman," she said as she started turning into a cloud of greed-dust. "There will always be a place in this world for the Grand Duchess of Greed."

The Grand Duchess completely transformed into greed-dust, and the wind carried her out through the open window of the shop. The Bibleteam and Lila watched with surprise.

"So villains can be sweet, old ladies now? What happened to villains looking like, well, villains?" Melody asked.

"You weren't the only one who was deceived today, Lila," Bibleman said. "The enemy can attack in almost any form. Even Satan disguises himself as an angel of light, but the Word of God is our light to lead us back to Christ."

"Thanks, Bibleman," Lila said. "I'll sell these at the fund-raiser and donate whatever I make."

Bibleman radioed Cypher to give him an update. "The Grand Duchess of Greed is gone, and we're going to the fund-raiser with one very generous girl."

Remember
"But when you give to the poor, don't let your left hand know what your right hand is doing, so that your giving may be in secret. And your Father who sees in secret will reward you."—Matthew 6:3–4

Read
Read Acts 20:35. The many treasures of life—toys, clothes, and games—can make it easy to focus on ourselves. We want more and more stuff for our own enjoyment and happiness. But Jesus tells us that what makes us happy isn't getting stuff for ourselves—it's giving stuff away to people who really need it! When we focus on ourselves, our reward is the tiny amount of things we have; when we focus on helping others and spreading God's love, He gives us rewards that will last forever and ever. We should always think of others before ourselves.

Think
1. When is a time you were greedy or wanted to keep something only for yourself?
2. What are three ways that you can be generous?
3. How many Bible verses can you find about generosity? (*Hint: start with Proverbs 11:24–25 and Luke 6:38.*)

Show God's love with generosity.